THE SOUL

OF A SINNER

Sammie Latroy Wells

WWW.TRUEVINEPUBLISHING.ORG

The Soul of a Sinner
By Sammie Latroy Wells

Published by
True Vine Publishing Co.
810 Dominican Dr.
Nashville, TN 37228
www.TrueVinePublishing.org

ISBN: 978-1-968092-22-1 Paperback
ISBN: 978-1-968092-23-8 eBook

Printed in the United States of America—First printing.

PROLOGUE

The steady drip… drip… drip of water from the kitchen faucet played in the back of Chaz-man's mind like a slow, hypnotic beat. He lay stretched out on the sagging mattress in the dimly lit, one-bedroom apartment in downtown Chicago, eyes half-closed, body heavy with the weight of sleep.

Tia was at her new job, leaving the apartment quiet except for the soft hum of the fridge and the occasional groan of the old building settling into its bones. The air was stale, carrying a faint smell of fried food from the neighbor's place downstairs.

A sudden chill snaked across his skin, slipping beneath his shirt. His eyes shot open. The breeze crept in through the slight opening of the window above the kitchen sink, rustling the edge of a paper bag on the counter.

He sat up, heart kicking into a quicker rhythm. No time to think. Just move. He swung his legs off the bed, feet finding the cold floor, and in a flash, he was at the door, yanking it open and heading for the car.

The streets outside were calm, traffic gliding by in an unhurried rhythm as he steered toward the library. The plan was simple: get online, handle business.

Then it happened. The first burst of gunfire cracked the air like fireworks far too close. Another volley followed, then another, sharp, deafening pops coming from nearly every direction. His chest tightened, pulse roaring in his ears.

"Shit!" he hissed, stomping the gas pedal.

The Hyundai leapt forward. His grip tightened on the wheel, knuckles white. Too late.

From the corner of his eye, a hulking shape emerged. An eighteen-wheeler, bearing down. The impact hit like a freight train, metal shrieking as the Sonata crumpled under the force. The world spun violently; the car flipped, weightless for a split second before slamming into a telegraph pole.

Glass exploded. Gasoline poured from the wreckage, its sharp scent mixing with the acrid bite of burning wires. Overhead, power lines snapped and spat sparks, each one flirting dangerously with the spreading puddle of fuel.

Chaz-man's world went black.

He didn't hear the sirens. He didn't feel the hands pulling at the twisted frame. The paramedics' shouts, the metallic groan of the jaws of life, the rush of air as they pried him free. All of it was lost to the darkness.

When the helicopter's rotors finally thundered overhead, he was still out cold. They loaded him in and rushed him to the hospital. Surgery came next. Then the quiet, relentless beeping of machines in the ICU.

TABLE OF CONTENTS

CHAPTER 1

Six months had crawled by with Chaz-man trapped in the sterile chokehold of the hospital. The sharp, chemical bite of antiseptic never left his nostrils, no matter how many times the nurses cracked the window to let in a thin breath of winter air. Physical therapy was its own warzone; every push of his legs sent white-hot lightning through both shattered thighs, and each deep inhale made his four broken ribs groan like rusted hinges. The worst was the constant, throbbing reminder of the deep gash in his pelvis, the one that nearly bled him dry.

The streets hadn't gone quiet about it either. Word shot through Chicago faster than any siren. "Mohawk did it," they said in hushed tones over card games, in barbershops thick with talcum powder and aftershave, in backseats where the air was clouded with blunt smoke. Mohawk, the grimy dude with the snitch label who, according to the word on the curb, called the police on people just for kicks. No one knew how he got his name. Didn't matter. If the rumor was truth, Mohawk had just signed his own death certificate.

Through all of it, Tina had been there. Almost five years together had weathered them through worse, but this? This was different. Every night for half a year, she'd curled herself into the lumpy couch in his hospital room, her soft snore blending with the steady beep of the heart monitor. She only left to grab a quick shower, swap into clean clothes, and sometimes handle business for him on the outside. The circles under her eyes told their own story.

March 26, 2009, the day he finally touched the outside world again. The cold air hit his face like freedom, though his body still ached from the inside out. He'd missed Thanksgiving, Christmas, New Year's. All that, but none of that mattered. He was alive, and now all he wanted was to find the man who had almost killed him.

The cab ride home was quiet, the kind of silence that left space for dangerous thoughts. His eyes drifted to the city sliding past the window, flickering liquor store signs, kids in hoodies posted on corners, the same streets he'd bled for. His mind kept circling back to the apartment Tina had managed to lock down with what little cash he'd had stashed. Not the kind of spot he was used to, but better than the one-bedroom they'd left behind. Two bedrooms now. More room for him to set up shop with a tattoo chair or whatever hustle he decided to run.

It hadn't been long since his last stretch. Just over a year ago he'd walked out of prison, fresh off serving 120 days for traffic tickets that stacked higher than the law allowed in county. By the time he came back, the job he'd held, cleaning boilers and pipe systems in paper and steel mills was long gone.

Starting over from zero was a grind. His job searches hit dead ends, and when he wasn't home in a shouting match with Tina, he was up the block. Big Will. Travis. Ronald and Donald, the twins. And D.A., the slick-talking scam artist who could pull money out of thin air and trouble out of nowhere.

One evening, out of the blue, Chaz-man's phone rang. To his surprise, it was Travis on the other end, saying he had a mission for him. All Chaz had to do was ride along with one of Travis's friends, a guy named Flip, and when the moment came, Chaz would know exactly what to do.

They agreed to meet at a designated location at 8:30 p.m., thirty-five minutes away. Once there, Travis gave a quick, no-nonsense briefing, then went his separate way, leaving Chaz and Flip to set out on the ride.

They cruised down a long, deserted road when, without warning, Flip yanked up the emergency brake. The minivan spun out wildly, tires screaming as it swerved in a dizzy spiral before nose-diving into a ditch. When the van finally stopped, the smell of burned rubber lingered in the air. Flip smirked and said, "Damn, did you see that fucking deer?"

Chaz knew instantly that this was a quick come-up scheme.

As they climbed out of the van, headlights appeared behind them. A passerby pulled over, leaning out to ask if they were okay and what caused the crash. Immediately, the role-play kicked in. Chaz and Flip grabbed at different parts of their bodies, groaning, claiming a deer had darted out in front of them and forced them off the road.

While the good Samaritan was on the phone giving the accident location to 911, Chaz and Flip quietly made sure their stories matched, crossing their T's and dotting their I's.

It felt like forever before the ambulance, tow truck, and several police units arrived. The cops and EMS repeated the same questions over and over before finally loading Chaz and Flip into the ambulance. The ride to the hospital felt like a straight shot toward a big payday neither had to break a sweat for.

In the ER, doctors ran every test and X-ray they could think of. Both men were discharged in the early hours of the morning, though at different times.

A few days later came the next step: picking up a copy of the incident report from the police department and notifying the insurance company about the claim against the van's owner. Then followed a series of "doctor visits" at different hospitals around the state, stacking up expensive tests so the insurance payout would be as fat as possible.

About a month later, Chaz's patience paid off. He cashed a check for $19,000, peeling off $2,000 for Travis as thanks for putting him in on the play.

Flip, on the other hand, didn't tell Travis or Chaz how much he got paid. He decided, "Fuck it," and disappeared with his money. Travis didn't care; he had other insurance settlements lined up like clockwork. Flip was just another lesson learned.

On the way to cash his check, Chaz had been browsing the internet for motorcycles when one caught his eye, matte black, chromed out to the fullest, a 2003 Honda VT 1100 listed for $3,500. He immediately called the seller to set up a meeting, hoping he'd be able to ride it home that same day if things went well.

Not even thirty minutes after cashing the check, Chaz was on his way home on his new motorcycle to get the title transferred, insurance in place, and license tags squared away.

"Damn, so you got one already?" Travis asked, his eyes glued to the bike.

"Hell yeah! You know I gotta get me one."

"Yeah, I know," said Chaz. "Take it around the block, see what it does."

It had been a long time since Chaz had real money in his hands, and he was determined to keep the flow steady. He decided to partner with Travis and go half on an apartment they could use to sell alcohol, cigarettes, cigars, sodas, snacks; whatever the local community needed, especially for folks without transportation to a store.

The only problem was, Travis's scam money hadn't come in yet, so Chaz put up all the initial funding. They secured a three-bedroom apartment and stocked it top to bottom with every kind of beer and liquor imaginable, closets packed to avoid constant store runs. Their prices undercut everyone in town. Half-pints moved quick for individual sales, while 1.75-liter bottles kept the shot glasses full.

Other sellers charged fifty cents per loose cigarette or three for a dollar. Chaz had the business sense to order cartons in bulk from China: ten cartons for $400 instead of four for $200, making it impossible for anyone else in the neighborhood to compete. Cigarette sales alone brought in over 35% of their profit.

Chaz ran the spot in the mornings but left around 10 p.m., heading home to his woman and child while Travis handled the night shift. The problem was,

Travis had other priorities: blowing money, chasing nightlife, and selling multiple types of drugs.

Eventually, Chaz hired a local kid named Shy to stay overnight and catch late sales. Shy had a sidekick named Young, who spent most of his time chain-smoking blunts.

Meanwhile, Travis grew reckless, letting all kinds of random people hang around outside, doing whatever they wanted. He turned his part of the operation into a weed and cocaine house, drawing in the kind of traffic that got neighbors whispering and cops cruising by more often.

To make matters worse, Travis never paid his share of the expenses but still came through late at night to collect money from Shy and Young. The final straw came when Chaz asked for the alcohol and tobacco sales money and Travis shrugged.

"Man, I was trickin' with this chick, Shawty-Redd, and when I went to sleep, she took $400 out my pocket."

"So you're telling me that was my $400 she took?" Chaz asked, his voice low.

"Pretty much," Travis sighed. "But we'll figure something out."

Chaz could feel himself turning into a ticking time bomb.

One day, his ten-year-old son Marquise, who had been visiting for the summer and ended up staying, said

"Daddy, Aaron asked me to walk with him to get some free sodas from his uncle like he does every day. But when we got there, it was your house, and he gave us two sodas each and some snacks."

Chaz's jaw tightened. Without a word, he grabbed his keys and headed straight to the spot, ready to confront Shy. When he arrived, Shy was nowhere to be found, the back door wide open like an invitation. Chaz waited.

When Shy finally walked in, Chaz exploded. "You motherfucka! Since you wanna give my shit away, go back and live with your fucking grandma."

Shy was out.

Chaz had just about had it with Travis, too. He texted him to meet at the spot ASAP, because whatever they had wasn't a partnership, it was Chaz funding everything while Travis played games.

When Travis showed up, he leaned back in his chair like nothing was wrong. "You think you can handle the spot financially on your own?"

"Is that a trick question? I'm doing that now," Chaz shot back.

Without another word, Travis reached into his pocket and pulled out the house key wrapped in a five-dollar bill; payment for a bottle of liquor he'd drunk the night before.

With that, all the loose ends were tied up. Chaz was running his one-man operation the way he should have from the beginning.

CHAPTER 2

Word was all over Chi-Town that Big Will had been arrested for allegedly shooting at a snitch named Rome. When the police pulled Big Will's car over, they found a substantial quantity of drugs in his possession. How much and what kind didn't matter. Everybody in the hood knew Rome was a confidential informant and nowhere near Big Will's favorite cup of tea.

As the story went, Chaz and Big Will were hanging on the corner at Brenda's house when Rome rolled up asking to buy some weed. Big Will looked him dead in the face and said, "*Nah, I don't fuck* with you! You got me caught up with that distribution charge a few years back."

The two went back and forth, words getting heated, but nothing popped off right then. Not long after, Rome got shot by somebody. Knowing the type of dude Rome was and how reckless he carried himself, he probably ran his mouth to the wrong person and ended up with hot lead pumped in his ass.

What better way for Rome to get back at Big Will than to point the finger and accuse him of being the shooter?

Tasha, Big Will's girl, was ride-or-die. She handled all the bond paperwork, scraped up money from family, friends, and whatever other sources she could tap. About a week after the arrest, Tina and Chaz were driving past Big Will's house when they spotted him and Tasha standing in the front yard. They stopped immediately, and in seconds Chaz was out of the car, giving Big Will a "welcome home, homie" hug.

Without hesitation, Chaz reached into his pocket, pulled out two crispy $100 bills, and handed them over. "Get your money up. Don't worry about paying me back," he told him.

Just as quick as he'd stepped out, Chaz was back in the car with Tina, grinning from ear to ear the whole ride home.

***

The backyard was packed with people buying everything from beers to blunt wraps. Chaz had a table set up under a tent, and Marie, the girl from next door, was frying up chicken wings and tilapia baskets, selling them with sodas. Everybody was having a good time, and business was moving steady for Chaz.

D.A. had once shown up at the spot with a pocket full of cash, but by the time he left, he was staring at the ground with empty pockets. From that day on, he started calling the spot "Ground Zero."

Even though Travis was no longer part of Ground Zero's day-to-day operations, people still came looking for weed, since that had been a staple of his late-night hustle. Every now and then, Chaz would grab a package or two to catch the loose weed money that still trickled through.

One of those weed customers ended up renting the vacant apartment next door, which had been empty since Chaz opened shop. Her name was Kim. She wasn't all there, but now she was his new neighbor. Chaz cut her some slack, let her open a tab since her son played on the same football team as his boy, even letting the kid ride to and from practice and games without asking for gas money.

Kim would pop over for single cigarettes, hang around for free drinks, and smoke off every blunt that got passed. She got so comfortable that she started stopping customers headed to Chaz's, telling them, "Chaz said if you're looking for cigarettes, get them from me. He doesn't want to be bothered."

That game caught up to her when she pulled it with Brenda. Brenda just looked at her like she was talking to herself and walked straight to Chaz's to let him know what Kim was trying to pull. Chaz didn't care about her selling cigarettes, it was the lie about him not wanting to be bothered that pissed him off.

To make sure she was running the hustle, he sent Brenda over with a dollar for two cigarettes. Peeking from the door, Chaz watched Kim get up, walk into her place, and come back with exactly what Brenda asked for.

Since she was already $30 deep in debt to him, Chaz told her, "Since you're selling cigarettes now, you can afford some gas money and to pay something on your bill."

That crazy bitch told him to "get your money the best way you know how" and shut the door in his face. Right then, Chaz decided to cut her off, not just the little debt, but her son's free rides, too.

The next day, two people came back-to-back to buy cigarettes from GROUND ZERO. When Chaz opened the door for the third knock, it was the landlord asking for him. When Chaz confirmed, the landlord went off, yelling, "I sat outside and watched two cars pull up back-to-back. I know a dope house when I see one. The neighbor says you've got traffic in and out all day and night. I want you out of here!"

Chaz grinned. "I'll leave as soon as you evict me." Then he slammed the door before the landlord could get another word out.

A couple minutes later, Chaz peeked out the window and saw the landlord still sitting in front of the mailbox on his phone. He stepped outside, climbed onto his motorcycle, and fired it up before riding off to Big Will's to fill him in on what had just gone down.

***

Tina was in the kitchen washing dishes when Chaz walked in the house. Everything seemed calm, then out of nowhere, she started screaming at the top of her lungs, asking him why in the fuck Kim had texted her saying he'd eaten her pussy.

She was furious, her voice sharp enough to cut glass. "Why in the fuck would Kim text me saying you ate her pussy?" Tina shouted, slamming the dish she was rinsing back into the sink so hard that water splashed onto the counter.

Chaz held his hands up, palms out. "Tina, that shit never happened. She's lying. You know how she is, always looking for some way to stir up drama."

"Don't play with me, Chaz," she shot back, eyes locked on him. "Kim said it like it was straight facts. She even went into detail."

Chaz shook his head. "Details? She can make up all the stories she wants. I haven't touched her, and you know damn well if I did, I wouldn't be stupid enough to let it get back to you like this. She's mad 'cause I cut her off, that's all this is."

Tina crossed her arms, glaring at him. "So you're telling me she just made this up out of nowhere?"

"Exactly," he said firmly. "She's trying to get between us because she can't use me anymore. She's petty like that."

Tina grabbed her phone, scrolled through the text, and then muttered, "I just find it hard to believe you'd go down on her and not get anything in return. That's what don't make sense to me."

Chaz leaned in, meeting her eyes. "Because it didn't happen, Tina. Think about it: does anything she says really add up? This is Kim we're talking about."

Tina studied his face for a long moment, searching for any sign he was lying. Finally, she sighed, the tension in her shoulders loosening. "Yeah… the whole thing sounds off. She's been on some bullshit for a while now."

"That's what I've been trying to tell you," Chaz replied. "Let her run her mouth. It's all she's got."

After thinking it over, Tina decided the story didn't add up at all, and that was the last time the subject ever came up.

About three weeks later, the eviction notice Chaz had requested was finally issued by the police. As he held the paperwork in his hand, he turned to Tina and said, "That's it. I'm shutting down Ground Zero. I'm done with the drama. Time to stay home, be with my family, and make some honest money."

Tina nodded, a small smile breaking through. "Good. That's the smartest thing I've heard you say in a long time."

CHAPTER 3

"In the case of the State of Illinois vs. Dal-Venus Upchurch on the charge of *Criminal Sexual Conduct, 1st Degree*, Mr. Upchurch, you have been found guilty by a jury of your peers and are hereby sentenced to serve 18 years in the Illinois Department of Corrections at Fallgate Correctional Institution without the possibility of parole. Good luck."

After what seemed like a month or more, it had only been two weeks since Dal-Venus was convicted for the malicious rape of Queenie McVeil. Word traveled like wildfire through Fallgate Correctional Institution: he had just hit the yard.

D-Block was almost certain to be his home for the next 18 years; the same unit that housed some of the most violent inmates in the facility.

Zeek was there on a probation violation for ABHAN: assault and battery of a high and aggravated nature. He also had pending charges for attempted murder and attempted armed robbery, waiting to stand trial. That's what landed him at Fallgate.

Rooster had grown up with Zeek on the streets of the South Side. He was serving 30 years to life for the kidnapping and brutal murder of Zoe, a crackhead who broke into his stash house and stole three ounces of black-tar heroin. Rooster snatched him off the street late one night, dragged him to a public park, and tied him to a flagpole. After beating Zoe for nearly 30 minutes and getting no answers, Rooster knocked him out cold with the butt of his 9mm Beretta, drenched him in gasoline, and set him ablaze with the cigarette he'd been smoking seconds before. Zoe's body convulsed violently as the flames devoured his flesh. His screams could be heard for half a mile, if anyone was listening. Rooster might have gotten away with it if not for park surveillance footage from prior vandalism incidents.

Midnight was serving 3–5 years for ABHAN as well. The son of a South Carolina farmer, he had migrated to Chicago with a truckload of produce and a goat as his companion. He rented a basement from an elderly couple, who soon reported disturbing noises that sounded like an animal being tortured. When police arrived, they found Midnight pacing the floor, drenched in sweat, with what appeared to be semen dripping from his penis. The same fluid mixed with blood was visible on the goat's vagina.

This was enough for police to arrest him for sexual misconduct with an animal. That charge was later dismissed, but not before he severely beat another inmate who kept calling him a "goat fucker from Carolina." That fight landed him in Fallgate for two more years.

Jack Mack had been a small-time weed dealer who decided to upgrade to selling cocaine. He never had the funds to buy a kilogram, but a partner put him on to synthetic cocaine: cheap, but giving users similar effects. Jack Mack jumped in headfirst selling the fake product. His downfall came when he tried to expand by paying a correctional officer to smuggle two ounces into Fallgate for his brother Odie, who was already serving 12 years for voluntary manslaughter after a drug deal shootout.

What Jack Mack didn't know was the guard had been under federal investigation. When caught, the guard cut a deal to avoid a 15-year federal sentence by giving up his supplier, Jack Mack. The two had always met at 2:00 p.m. sharp on Saturdays at a bench outside the public library. One day, after the guard walked away, sirens wailed and unmarked cars swarmed the area. FBI agents in blue and yellow jackets poured out, and Jack Mack knew he was fucked.

But the bust wasn't as bad as it could have been. The "cocaine" turned out to be *procaine*, an imitation.

That dropped his sentence from 15 years federal to 5 years state, landing him in Fallgate with Odie.

Goat was serving 10 years as a repeat offender for crack possession. Doing time was nothing new for him. This was far from his first bid, but this stretch would be different. Dal-Venus Upchurch was the reason. It was Upchurch who raped Goat's wife, Queenie McVeil.

Rooster, Zeek, Jack Mack, Odie, and Goat had all grown up in the same neighborhood. They knew each other since grade school, and now, the man who had violated the wife of one of their own was being delivered right on their doorstep.

Everyone knew Dal-Venus would be housed in D-Block, right alongside them. In D-Block, there was only one rule: everything gets eaten in the jungle.

***

Almost two months had passed since the arrival of Dal-Venus Upchurch. Coming from Detroit, Michigan, and only moving to Chicago after Goat had been locked up, he didn't have a clue who the hell Goat was.

It was getting close to time for Zeek to max out, but that didn't mean shit to him. The smell of sweet revenge was in the air. His custody level had recently dropped from Level 5 to Level 4, meaning he was no longer considered maximum security.

One afternoon, while elbow-deep in a tub of soapy water, scrubbing trays in the kitchen and getting ready to return to the unit, Zeek heard his number called over the loudspeaker. The loudspeaker cracked to life overhead.

"Inmate four-seven-two-one-nine, report to Operations on the main yard. Inmate four-seven-two-one-nine, report to Operations."

He froze mid-scrub, glancing up like the ceiling might explain itself.

"The fuck they want with me now?"

A kitchen worker two stations down snorted, "Maybe you pissed somebody off again."

"Nah… I ain't done shit lately."

The cook smirked, "Yet."

He tossed the tray onto the rack, water sloshing onto the floor. Drying his hands on his pants, he muttered under his breath. "Hell, for all I know, they could be shippin' me out. But they better have a damn good reason."

With that, he left the kitchen, his mind running through every possible reason why Operations wanted him.

When he arrived, the blow hit hard: he was being transferred to a lower-level penitentiary the next morning. Zeek rushed back to the unit to tell the fellas. They were disappointed he was leaving before his max-out date, but at the same time, relieved. He only had two months left before he was a free man, and they weren't about to let him fuck that up by being involved in the gruesome plans they had for Dal-Venus Upchurch.

Rooster, the best wine maker in the unit, always kept gallons on deck and was drunk most of the time anyway. This news was just another excuse for a celebration. As the drinking session kicked off, Midnight kept reminiscing about his southern upbringing and farm life.

Rooster went on and on about cooking crack and the money he made at his trap house. Odie didn't say much, he was too busy being a horny dog, counting down the days until he could get back to society and fuck everything that moved. He was already perving on every female officer who stood still long enough to make eye contact while he had his dick in his hand. If she didn't break her stare, he'd jerk all the way off. In his twisted mind, you couldn't convince him he hadn't just had sex with the woman of his dreams.

Goat, on the other hand, couldn't wait to reunite with Queenie after ten years and to make Dal-Venus Upchurch scream in pain like no human had ever screamed before.

Jack Mack was a pure fuck*ing hater on the low, and when he was drunk, his true colors bled through. He'd take little shots, saying, "All you gonna do is go home and bring* *your ass right back for some dumb* shit." Nobody cared. Everyone knew that's just how he was.

Zeek, though, was ready to leave the shot-caller version of himself behind in prison where it belonged, and step back into life on the outside: back to basics, but with a touch of class.

CHAPTER 4

Although years had passed since her husband endured a severe, life-altering experience, the nightmarish screams continued. Time and time again, Chastity would be jolted awake in the middle of the night by the sound of her husband being tormented in his dreams. Whatever he had gone through, he never spoke of it.

Chastity understood the silence. Growing up, she had endured her own hellish experiences: things she would never speak of to anyone. So, she didn't pry. She didn't meddle. She was just there, wrapping her arms around him in the dark whenever the nightmares came.

After numerous failed attempts at making an honest living, and with tax season rolling around again, Chaz decided to try his hand in the streets once more. He found a vacant apartment in the neighborhood, paid the security deposit and first month's rent, then stocked it with everything he needed to turn it into one of the most prosperous after-hours hangout spots in the city—more like an underground operation.

He bought a pound of weed, every brand of liquor he could think of, and an assortment of cigarillos, cigarettes, and cigars for black-market sales. Word spread fast. Soon, everybody in the hood was stopping by to buy something. People even came through to sell him items at dirt-cheap prices when they needed quick cash. If it was something he liked, he'd buy it.

Some nights got so crowded, the line of customers stretched from the kitchen to the front door. Big Will often came by to help keep the flow steady. His specialty? Smoking loud, drinking Paul Masson, popping Molly, and clowning on people. He and Chaz had an unspoken brotherly bond. In their neighborhood, they were in a league of their own. They were considered five-star generals. They made money, got shit done, and when they spoke, people listened. Almost nothing went down in the hood without one of them being informed, either before it happened or shortly after.

***

"Damn, can't you just turn that fuck*ing phone off when you're at home? That shit* was ringing all night while you were sleeping, and it woke me up this morning!" Tina yelled as she got dressed for work.

Chaz smirked, half-asleep, and reached for his phone. "Damn… 37 missed calls?" The last one had come in minutes ago; probably the one Tina was complaining about.

It was business as usual, but maybe he *did* need to silence his calls when he was home. He stretched, yawned, and headed to the bathroom to take a leak, brush his teeth, and shower.

Later, sliding into the driver's seat of a Mazda 626, he thought, *This ain't like my Sonata…* But the A/C worked, and the music was hitting just as hard as in his old ride. He shifted into reverse, ready to back out, when Tina appeared in the doorway holding his phone, shaking it playfully.

"You were about to leave this," she teased.

Chaz hopped out, grabbed the phone, and gave her a quick kiss. As he stepped off the porch, the phone rang again.

"Hello?" he answered.

"Yeah… I'll be there in a few."

And just like that, his day began.

***

"Your mother's breast cancer has returned. This time more aggressive, and her chances of survival aren't looking good. You need to come home."

Chastity sat on the side of the bed, sobbing, after hanging up the phone with her father. Her husband was never a people person, and he insisted she go alone to handle whatever family affairs were necessary.

The trip home felt empty and lonely. Cincinnati, as she had left it years ago, was still the same. Two days after she arrived, her mother passed away. In those final hours, they talked about everything from Chastity's childhood to her mother's untimely departure. But before she died, her mother revealed something that shook Chastity to her core, something she never expected to hear.

As Chastity sat at her mother's bedside, holding her frail hand, Opal's voice came low and uneven.

"Baby… there's something I should've told you a long time ago."

Chastity leaned in, her brows knitting together. "What is it, Mama?"

Opal took a slow, shallow breath. "You… you weren't born to me and Larry. We adopted you when you were just a baby."

The words hit Chastity like a punch to the chest. "What do you mean… adopted? Mama, what are you talking about?"

Opal's eyes watered. "Your real parents' names were Tyrone and Odessa Croswell. They were from Chicago, Illinois."

Chastity stared at her in disbelief. "Are they... are they still alive?"

Her mother hesitated, her gaze shifting to the ceiling as if searching for the right words. "Your mother—your biological mother—died seventeen years ago while serving a life sentence... for the murder of your father."

Chastity felt her throat tighten. "So... they're both gone?"

Opal gave a faint nod. "Yes, baby. They're gone."

Chastity squeezed her mother's hand, her mind spinning. "All this time... and you never told me?"

"I thought I was protecting you," Opal whispered. "I wanted you to grow up knowing love... not the pain they left behind."

"Whew," she sighed softly to herself. *At least they were married.*

Chastity spent the next two weeks with Larry Banks, the man she had known as her father for the past 35 years and who would always be her father in her heart. One afternoon, Larry handed her an envelope.

She opened it and gasped. "Daddy... this is—"

"Don't say a word, baby," he interrupted gently. "Your mother's life insurance policy settled. I split the remainder between the two of us." He wrapped his arms around her, and they both sobbed quietly.

They both knew this was the beginning of one life and the end of another for her.

The line at the Birth Records window moved quickly. Only three people stood ahead of Chastity. The woman behind the glass, a short, salt-and-pepper-haired lady, worked with quick precision. Within minutes, Chastity stood before her.

Her name tag read Yolanda Brock. She looked about forty-five, brown-skinned, with two perfectly straight rows of teeth that hinted at dentures.

"May I help you?" Yolanda asked.

"Yes," Chastity began. "I was adopted as a child by Larry and Opal Banks, but my birth parents were Tyrone and Odessa Croswell. My name at birth was Chastity Croswell. I'm here to obtain all birth records under that name."

Yolanda began typing. The rhythmic tapping of keys filled the pause before she looked up. "That will be $16. It'll take three days for your request to be processed."

"That's fine," Chastity replied, sliding a crisp twenty-dollar bill through the opening and waiting for her change and receipt.

***

One Friday afternoon, riding through the Windy City, Chaz's mind clicked onto a new money-making idea. Instead of passing by as he had countless times before, he flipped on his turn signal at the last second and made a hard right into City Title Loans.

Inside the lot, his eyes landed on two cars: a 2002 white Mitsubishi Galant and a 1997 winter-green Ford Thunderbird. Each was priced at $500. After a brief conversation with the manager, Todd Biggs, Chaz handed over $1,000, got the titles, and drove off as quickly as he had pulled in.

Immediately, he called Travis to help transport the cars back to the hood, one at a time. To avoid vandalism, Chaz rented two storage units to keep them secure. Once the cars were safely tucked away, he snapped photos and listed them on Chicago's Craigslist and a couple of other sites.

By the next morning, his phone was blowing up. It had started raining, so he arranged for all potential buyers to meet him the following day. As soon as the storage business opened, it didn't take long. Within minutes, both cars were sold for $1,500 each.

***

Chasity's mind had been racing a hundred miles an hour since she learned the truth about her real parents. Today felt like the first day of school, but it was actually the day she'd been counting down to since filing the paperwork at the Department of Social Services. Her birth records were finally ready for pickup.

She grabbed her keys from the kitchen counter and started toward the door. That's when she felt the firm, all-too-familiar grip of her husband's hand clamp around her wrist.

"Where the hell do you think you're going?" he roared, his voice monstrous and full of rage.

Before she could answer, the inside palm of his right hand came crashing down across the left side of her jaw, knocking her weightlessly to the floor. Darkness swallowed her.

A sudden splash of cold water shocked her back into consciousness. She groaned, running the back of her right hand over her aching jaw. When she looked, there was a smear of dark red blood across her skin.

Her worst nightmare had just stepped into reality. The man she once loved had become the monster she'd been refusing to believe he was turning into these past few weeks. Out of fear that he'd take things further, she crawled into bed, curled into the fetal position, and cried herself to sleep.

***

It had been a long-ass day for Chaz; nonstop ripping and running the streets. His expression said *What now?* as Tina walked toward the car before he could even close the door behind him. She held a tiny piece of paper in her hand.

As she handed it over, she said, "His name's Midnight."

A quick conversation later, just enough time to get the man's address, and a week had passed. Chaz was on his way to South Carolina to visit the blackest dude he knew. Midnight was a true southerner at heart. Almost every sentence he spoke started or ended with the same phrase: "Talk-about, talk-bout." He was one of a kind. The type of man old folks meant when they said, "They don't make 'em like that no more."

Coming from the city, the endless twists and turns of those long country roads felt like a maze. Finally, Chaz pulled into the first yard he'd seen in fifteen minutes. Goats, chickens, and hogs milled about, each kept in its own space. A huge two-story farmhouse sat in the middle of it all, flanked by two massive tractors, an old red pickup that read Higgin's Produce on both doors, and acres of corn stretching to the horizon.

The narrow dirt road had kicked up a thick cloud of dust behind him. Standing behind the nearly blackened screen door was nothing but a set of white teeth and two eyes watching him.

His gut told him it was Midnight.

"Well, well, well! Talk-about, talk-bout. I see you made it, Zeek."

"Damn," Chaz chuckled, "I ain't been called that in years."

"You'll always be Zeek to me," Midnight grinned. "So… this country enough for you?"

"Hell yeah. So y'all grow everything you eat out here and sew your own clothes too?" Chaz laughed.

"Hell no. You a funny motherfucka, Zeek. We got stores and shopping centers. I just happen to live out here. You act like you ain't never been outside Chicago."

"Actually, I haven't. And had you not been a nigga I fuck with, my ass would still be in Chicago. So pipe it down, shit-stain shorty!"

"Man, fuck you, Zeek," Midnight shot back, laughing.

After a few more jabs and jokes, the ice between them melted. They drove into town, an hour away, and decided to hit Applebee's. Over drinks, they started swapping stories and reminiscing about their wildest times back at Fallgate.

***

Later that afternoon, Chastity woke up with a headache that felt like an elephant was standing on her head. Her husband was nowhere to be found; probably out bar-hopping, trying to drink away the

41

pain from his past. His whereabouts didn't matter to her.

Her focus was on getting to the bathroom to check her reflection, to make sure her face wasn't disfigured and she still looked decent enough to head downtown to pick up her paperwork from the DSS office before they closed. She was dying to know who she really was and start tracking down her family.

The only visible mark was the puffiness around her eyes from crying. Everything else, internal, still hurt like hell.

"Aww, Mrs. Croswell," said the same woman behind the glass as before.

"Hello, Mrs. Brock," Chastity replied.

It took her a few seconds to respond. She wasn't used to being called Mrs. Croswell, but when she did, it was with the biggest smile she'd worn in a long time.

Right there, she began to consider the possibility of leaving her husband. Silently, she swore on her biological parents' graves: if he ever laid a hand on her again, that would be the day his soul left his body. She would be the best thing that ever happened to him, but she would also be the last face he ever saw.

***

"So, tell me," Chaz asked over his drink, "what became of the rest of the niggas at Fallgate? You been in touch with anybody else besides me?"

"No," Midnight said, shaking his head. "I got transferred to a pre-release facility shortly after you left. What I *do* know is the rest of the guys got shipped out to different joints across the state."

"Why? What happened?" Chaz asked.

Midnight leaned in with a smirk. "Oh, you didn't know? We fucked that dude up—the one who raped Goat's old lady."

"Damn Chaz muttered. "Another nigga raped Queenie too?"

"No, the same niggaa—Dal-Venus Upchurch."

Chaz's brow furrowed. "How in the hell was that possible? I did his ass in the night before I left."

Midnight's eyes lit up. "Oh, so that *was* your handiwork. We figured you had something to do with it, but the only person who knew for sure—other than you—was him. You gutted that nigga bad, but he must've had nine lives, 'cause he survived."

Chaz slammed his glass down. "What the fuck you mean he survived?"

"Somehow, he gathered his guts, literally, in his arms and made it to the main lobby before collapsing in front of the officer's cage. But check this shit out… after he recovered, we tied him to the barber's chair, scalped him with a potato peeler from the kitchen, and stabbed that bitch over seventy-five times. His screams were so loud they echoed across the whole yard, so Rooster put him in a chokehold to shut him up while the rest of us kept stabbing."

Midnight shrugged. "Don't know if he passed out from being choked or losing blood. Either way, that shit locked the whole prison down for six months. Lucky for me, I was shipped to pre-release a couple days into the lockdown."

He leaned back. "A couple months later, another dude came in from Fallgate and told me Upchurch survived *that* too. Sued the state of Illinois in the Supreme Court and won. Been out a couple years now. They cut his sentence down to six years and sent him to minimum security."

Midnight's tone darkened. "But not before they convicted Goat for kidnapping and attempted murder. Natural life. Prosecutor was pissed he wouldn't admit to his part in it, and he wouldn't give up anyone else either. We figure he only got convicted 'cause Upchurch sued and won."

Chaz sat back, his stomach turning at the thought that there might be a man walking around Chicago who he had once tried and failed to kill. The thought was short-lived, though. Chicago would be the last place a registered sex offender like Upchurch would want to show his face, knowing the kind of retaliation that could be waiting for him.

CHAPTER 5

The only living relative listed in her paperwork was a **C. Croswell**.

Her heart skipped. She had been a fraternal twin from birth.

Growing up, she'd always dreamed of having a brother or sister—someone to share secrets with, someone who truly understood her. Now, learning she had a twin was more than surprising; it was intriguing, almost surreal.

The question now was whether he was still alive.

She wasted no time. Flipping open the local phone book, she scanned for any *Croswell* listings in the city and surrounding areas. One book turned into several. By the end of the day, her search had pulled up eighty-two listings across the state of Illinois—but not a single one gave her the slightest clue about the man she was searching for.

Maybe, like her, her twin had been adopted and taken his parents' last name.

That night, she sat on the edge of her bed, bowed her head, and prayed. *God, if it's Your will, send me a sign. Show me the answers I've been searching for.*

When she opened her eyes, she felt lighter. She decided to turn it all over to God and let it go—at least for now.

But before closing that chapter completely, she made one last move. She logged into Facebook and typed out a post:

> "Searching for my twin brother. His first initial may be C, last name at birth was Croswell. Date of birth. If anyone has information, please reach out."

She added a few childhood photos: snapshots of her wide-eyed smile, hoping that somewhere out there, a man with the same eyes, the same features, might see them and recognize himself.

***

Chaz kept his phone off and never touched the radio the whole ride home. His mind was too heavy, barely able to process half the shit he'd learned during his weekend with Midnight.

One thing was clear; Midnight was a true, blue, bona fide nigga. He'd kept his word about staying in touch after getting out, and he knew how to lay on that southern hospitality thick.

That damn Sticky Pot and steamed okra? Hands down the best meal Chaz had ever tasted. The Sticky Pot was a mix of pig's feet, pigtails, and hog maws slow-cooked together, simmered until the gravy turned rich and thick on its own.

You couldn't just wipe your hands and mouth with a paper towel after eating it. Nah, you had to actually get up and wash your hands and face with a washcloth to get all that stickiness off.

Chaz was already thinking about making it for Tina when he got home or maybe letting her cook it for him. Didn't matter who was behind the stove, but it was non-negotiable that it be served over fluffy white rice with a side of hot Jiffy cornbread.

***

The sudden vibration under his tires, followed by a deep thudding noise, told Chaz he was drifting off the road. His chest tightened with panic, but he forced himself to stay calm, easing the wheel back into his lane instead of yanking it and risking a disaster.

Spotting a rest area sign two miles ahead, he decided to stop. When he finally pulled in, he stepped out into the cool night air, stretching his legs and shoulders. Inside the restroom, he splashed cold water on his face, relieved by the sharp jolt it gave him, then grabbed an energy drink loaded with enough caffeine to push him through the last stretch home.

Back in the driver's seat, he powered on his phone—9:30 p.m. He hadn't spoken to Tina since around eleven the night before. A quick call confirmed she was fine. With that reassurance, he popped in an old NOTORIOUS B.I.G. CD, letting the heavy beat of *I Got a Story to Tell* fill the car. The lyrics took him back to his younger days, when he'd run wild and pull off robberies like they were just another hustle.

By the time he rolled into his driveway, it was close to midnight. Marquis was long asleep, but Tina was still awake, waiting for him. From the corner of his eye, he caught the flicker of a candle in the bathroom, its glow reflecting off the steamy mountain of bubbles in the tub.

"Take off your clothes and get in," she said from the doorway, her voice low and inviting. "I'll wash your back."

He did so without hesitation, like an obedient child following a mother's instructions. Steam from the bath clung to his skin as he stepped out, the candle's faint light still flickering in the bathroom behind him. Once dried, he blew out the flame, plunging the room into darkness, and climbed into bed beside her warm, waiting body.

He reached through the dark, fingers brushing over the soft curves of her face, searching for her mouth. Their lips found each other—hungry, searching—and he slid his tongue deep, tasting her, drawing her in as if he could swallow her whole. She met him with equal fire, her own tongue pushing back, daring him.

She rolled over on top of him, her weight warm and steady. His hands slid down, cupping two full handfuls of her soft, petite ass. Beneath him, she could feel the urgent thump of his pulse racing through his rock-hard **dick**, pressing insistently against her hot, wet **pussy**. She shivered, then began to trail her tongue across his chest, slow and teasing, until her lips reached the base of his neck. Her left hand wrapped around his one-eyed monster as she lowered herself further, bringing her face closer to the waiting heat.

When her mouth finally closed over his **dick**, the room filled with the slick sound of her movements— wet, messy, deliberate. Every upstroke was punctuated with a deep, sloppy slurp, every downstroke with a guttural gag, as if she was punishing her own throat. He groaned, the sound low and primal.

Her saliva coated him completely, dripping past his balls, running over his skin. He guided her back onto the bed, lowering himself between her legs, and without pause began lapping at her **pussy** in slow, deliberate circles. The taste of her flooded his mouth as she arched her back, pressing upward as though she could feed him more. His fingers slid into her hairless heat, his lips locking over her clit, tongue flicking with steady precision.

Her breathing became ragged, her body trembling as wave after wave of orgasm crashed through her—five, maybe six in rapid fire—until she tugged him upward by his ears. "Now," she breathed. He didn't hesitate, guiding his boneless tube steak into her **pussy**.

The rhythm was relentless. He drove into her with her legs high on his shoulders, ankles crossed, pressing her back as far as she could go. The wet slap of their bodies filled the room, her release gushing down against his thighs like splashing water in a sink. She lay beneath him, helpless in pleasure, unable to stop the shudders that kept overtaking her.

He gripped her ankles, pinning her in place, pounding down harder, his massive hands wrapped around her legs. His large frame began to tense, muscles jerking as the edge drew near. With a growl, he grabbed the back of her hair, pulling her upright against the headboard. Standing slightly, he aimed his **dick** at her face, stroking it hard until he erupted, covering her mouth, chin, and cheeks in a hot rush.

She opened wide, sticking her tongue out so he could tap the tip of it with the head. Slowly, she rolled her tongue around him, wrapping her lips over the swollen head while her hand squeezed from the base to the tip, drinking down every last drop, just as she had many times before.

***

With the money she'd inherited from her mother's insurance policy, Chastity had grown accustomed to living alone in the one-bedroom apartment she'd been occupying for the past couple of weeks. Between work and adjusting to her new single lifestyle, she hadn't taken much time to dive deeper into her search for her twin.

Since moving in, she had purchased a small .25-caliber handgun and, after completing a few handgun safety courses, felt secure in her new space.

That evening, after a long hot shower and a roast beef sub, she decided to check her Facebook page to see if there had been any response to her post about finding her twin. But after a short search around her apartment, she realized she'd left her laptop at her husband's house.

She'd have to go back for it, only when she was sure he wouldn't be there. The spare key was still in her possession, but she intended to avoid a confrontation with him at all costs.

The notification popped up at the top of his screen, **Friend Request: Chastity Croswell**.

Chaz frowned, the name sticking in his head like a song lyric. He accepted without thinking and began scrolling through her profile.

No mutual friends.

An only child, according to her bio.

Birthday—**exactly** the same as his.

He blinked twice, leaning closer to the phone. "Same birthday? No way…" he muttered under his breath.

The room was quiet except for the low hum of the fridge in the corner. The pale blue light from the screen painted his hands, making his skin look almost ghostly.

Before he could process what he'd just seen, his phone buzzed violently in his palm– an incoming call. The jolt made him exhale sharply. He swiped to answer, carried on a quick, distracted conversation, then hung up. Another call flashed in before he could even set the phone down, but stopped ringing just as he lifted it to his ear.

The screen dimmed. He tapped it back awake. His Facebook feed still stared back at him.

A notification pulsed in red: **1 New Message**.

He didn't open it right away. His thumb hovered. Instead, he scrolled further down her wall. A post caught his eye, written in bold, aching letters:

"Searching for my twin brother. Separated at birth. If you're out there, please reach out. Birthday: August 14th. Born in Chicago. Last name at birth: Croswell."

A cold rush spread across his chest. The initials, C.C., were the same as his. But his last name? It wasn't even his parents' last name.

He leaned back, rubbing the back of his neck, staring at the glow of the screen. Seventeen questions crashed through his head at once, each louder than the last.

Finally, curiosity won. He tapped the blinking inbox icon.

The message opened.

And his mouth dropped.

"Hello Chazman, I know you don't have a clue in this world as to who I am, and I'm really not sure if you're who I think you are. It's a chance that you and I are fraternal twins, and I would like to take a DNA test to see if you're really my brother. All my life I've lived as an only child, but the lady I knew as my mother died a month ago, but not without giving me the information I needed to find my real family. If you're in fact my brother, we have so much to talk about, although a lifetime probably wouldn't be long enough to make up for our lost time.

Feel free to call me at (929)847-2234

Yours truly, Chastity

CHAPTER 6

HEADLINE NEWS:

Bright white lights from the CHANNEL 3 NEWS van splashed across the sand, casting long, distorted shadows toward the black waves rolling in. The faint sound of sirens carried in the distance, mixed with the low chatter of officers moving along the shoreline.

Reporter Kent Hurst stood in front of the camera, a Channel 3 mic gripped firmly in his right hand. His hair whipped in the cold wind, but his expression stayed grave.

"This makes the third victim in just three years," he began, his voice cutting through the sound of crashing waves, "found washed ashore with hands bound behind the back and naked."

He glanced down at his notes, the papers fluttering in the breeze. "All three victims were female, late twenties, close to thirty. Each was a single Black woman with a history of drug abuse."

A uniformed officer moved behind him, ducking out of the shot as Kent continued. "Although there are still no leads in the case, authorities have confirmed that each victim appears to have been strangled to death during intercourse."

The wind caught his tie, slapping it lightly against his jacket. He steadied it with one hand before looking directly into the lens.

"That's all we have for now, folks. This is Kent Hurst, reporting live from CHANNEL 3 NEWS. Thanks for tuning in."

The red light on the camera went dark. Kent exhaled, stepping away from the bright glare of the lens as the waves swallowed another gust of wind.

****

The phone had only rung three times before a soft, cautious whisper of a woman's voice came through the line.

"Hello?"

"Hi, this is Chaz… Chazman Croswell," he said, clearing his throat. "I'm calling about the message I got on Facebook from Chastity Croswell."

"Oh, hey, Chazman," she replied, her tone warming instantly. "Nice to finally hear your voice."

"Same to you," he said, forcing himself to keep his words light. The urge to launch into a barrage of questions burned in his chest, but he bit them back.

She paused for a beat, as if sensing his tension. "Look… would it be a problem if we met somewhere in person? I think it'd be better to talk face-to-face."

"No, that's fine," he said quickly. "You name the place and time, I'll be there."

"In that case," she said, her voice carrying a hint of excitement, "are you familiar with the east side of Chicago?"

"Sure," he replied without hesitation. "Where at?"

"I live at 7017 Beluga Ave," she said. "But I work twelve-hour shifts as a nurse at the children's hospital; on call twenty-four hours. My three days off for the week start when I get off Thursday night at seven o'clock. How's that?"

"That's perfect," he said, picturing the moment they'd lock eyes for the first time.

"Okay… guess it's a date," she said with a light laugh. "See you then, twin—I hope."

"Same here," he said, the corners of his mouth stretching into a grin he couldn't fight.

When they hung up, the quiet on both ends was electric. Each sat there for a moment longer, hearts beating a little faster, wondering if they had just found the missing link to their lives after so many years.

***

"Ah, so this bitch got a new car," he muttered under his breath. "Had me thinking she skipped town… but I got her ass now."

From a safe distance, he watched her step into the hospital parking garage and head toward a silver PT Cruiser. Same garage level, different ride. *Slick bitch.* He saw her point the remote, heard the faint beep, and watched the tail lights flash as she unlocked the car.

He eased his own vehicle forward, keeping three cars between them, just like in the detective movies, making sure she never caught on. Twenty minutes later, they were rolling through the east side of Chicago.

She turned down a narrow street. A green sign read **BELUGA AVE.** She parked, popped the trunk, and began pulling out bags. Still fumbling with her keys after locking the doors, she finally stepped inside.

Half a block away, he slid on black leather gloves, eyes fixed on the apartment she'd entered. He was halfway out of his car when headlights lit up his rearview mirror.

The hell…? He froze, watching the glow grow brighter until another vehicle pulled in right behind him. He sat there for a long minute. *What the fuck is this motherfucker doing?*

He was about to call it off when the driver's door opened. A man stepped out, walked right past him without so much as a glance, and headed straight for her door.

The sight made his blood boil. His first instinct was to jump out gun blazing, but he clenched the wheel and forced himself to breathe. *Unfuck*ing believable.

The man reached the door, knocked, and waited. The sound of locks turning carried down the street. That was it. He was done waiting.

Door barely closed behind him, he was already striding toward the apartment, gun drawn. The man at the door didn't even notice him until the cold steel pressed into his back. He shoved him forward, forcing him through the doorway.

"Surprise, surprise, bitches," he growled. "Looks like I'm not the only one who's hard to kill."

"Is this a fucking joke?" Chaz's voice cracked from the couch.

"Shut the fuck up, Zeek," the gunman barked.

"Who's Zeek, Chris?" Chastity asked, confusion written across her face.

"Who the fuck is Chris?" Chaz shot back.

"Both of you, shut the fu—"

Before he could finish speaking, the front door burst open with a crash. Heavy boots thundered inside.

"Get down! Don't move! Dal-Venus Upchurch, you're under arrest…"

The voice was loud, commanding. A tall man in plain clothes stood in the doorway, leather shoulder holster under his jacket, badge hanging from his belt.

"You two okay?" he asked, eyes darting between Chaz and Chastity.

Chastity's confusion deepened. "Who's Dal-Venus Upchurch?" she whispered.

It clicked for Chaz — the scarred scalp, the patch of hair sticking out like a flag. *Mohawk.* Midnight had told him about the potato-peeler scalping in South Carolina. The man with the gun had come back to settle the score.

Even stranger, the bastard had married Chaz's possible twin sister without even knowing it.

Upchurch was read his rights, cuffed, and escorted out to an unmarked cruiser.

The plainclothes detective stepped inside. "Detective Albert Wright," he introduced himself, voice calm but clipped. "Strange name for a white guy, I know."

He sat across from them, leaning forward. "Up until the most recent body washed ashore, we had nothing solid. All three victims; late 20s, single Black females, history of drug use. But cause of death wasn't overdose. All strangled during intercourse."

Chastity flinched.

"The first two times, the killer wore condoms. This last one? He didn't. Forensics got a semen sample, and within an hour we had a 100 percent DNA match to Dal-Venus Upchurch — convicted rapist. Problem was, he'd vanished after prison. Changed his name to Christopher Rheams."

The detective paused, looking straight at Chastity. "Married you."

Chastity's face went pale.

"We couldn't find an address, so we started tailing you from work. Saw you separated, figured there was trouble. Then we saw your Facebook search for your brother — and your messages with Chazman Croswell. Surveillance caught Upchurch circling your parking lot minutes before your shift ended. We put six cars on you. Used you as bait."

"Bait?" she snapped.

"Protocol," Wright said. "Best way to make sure he didn't panic and hurt someone."

When it was over, Wright stood and shook both their hands. "By the way — you two are biological brother and sister. I triple-checked. And you look just alike."

He smirked, walked to the door, and shut it behind him.

EPILOGUE

Over the next couple of months, Chastity and Chazman grew inseparable, making up for lost time and holding tight to the reality that they had almost missed each other completely. Life settled into a new rhythm with Tina, Marquis, Chazman, and Chastity doing things together as a family.

Dal-Venus Upchurch, also known as Christopher Reams and Mohawk, was found guilty on all charges and sentenced to three consecutive life sentences. As punishment for his heinous crimes and for mocking the state of Illinois by suing it before committing such acts against humanity, he was ordered to serve the rest of his life at Fallgate Correctional Institution.

When he was led down the corridor to the left wing of D-Block, his cellmate stood with his back turned, hunched over what appeared to be a drawing. The officer locked the cell door with a metallic click and walked away, chuckling to himself.

Goat turned slowly, smiling, holding the most jagged and vicious-looking shank imaginable. Upchurch knew instantly that calling for the guard was pointless. As Goat took two deliberate steps forward, the image of Queenie flashed in his mind, begging for help as Upchurch forced himself on her.

Gripping the blade with the point aimed downward, Goat lunged. Upchurch reached desperately for the weapon, but it was useless. His thumbs were severed in an instant as the shank plunged into his chest, tearing through bone and muscle until it burst from his back with the force of a roaring lion.

Goat yanked the blade free and came down again, this time on Upchurch's head. The strike split his right eye and socket, punched through the back of his skull, and ripped away the right side of his face. Goat withdrew the blade only to drive it down again and again.

The cell looked like the aftermath of a Jack the Ripper murder, with the walls, ceiling, and floor painted in gore. Compared to this, what Zeek had done to Upchurch years earlier was child's play.

When the officers finally entered the cell to escort Goat to solitary, Dal-Venus Upchurch lay sprawled in a puddle of blood, urine, and feces. His penis was shoved into his mouth, his testicles resting on his chin beside the shredded remains of his scrotum. The assault had lasted less than two minutes.

It was said that his screams could still be heard in the prison from time to time, the same chilling sound from the moment his soul was violently ripped from his body. Other than those ghostly cries, Dal-Venus Upchurch was never seen or heard from again.

www.ingramcontent.com/pod-product-compliance
Lightning Source LLC
Chambersburg PA
CBHW071206300726
48975CB00004B/1311